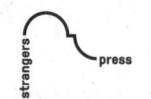

UEA PUBLISHING PROJECT
NORWICH

DIVORCE

KIM SOOM

Divorce
Kim Soom

Translated from the Korean by
Emily Yae Won

First published by
Strangers Press, Norwich, 2019
part of UEA Publishing Project

All rights reserved
Author © Kim Soom, 2019
Translator © Emily Yae Won, 2019

Distributed by
NBN International
10 Thornbury Road
Plymouth PL6 7PP
t. +44 (0)1752 202301
e.cservs@nbninternational.com

Printed by
Swallowtail, Norwich

Series editors
Nathan Hamilton & Deborah Smith

Editorial assistance
Senica Maltese

Cover design and typesetting
Glen Robinson

Illustration and Design Copyright © Glen Robinson, 2019

The rights of Kim Soom to be identified as the author and Emily Yae Won identified as the translator of this work have been asserted in accordance with the Copyright, Designs and Patents Act, 1988. This booklet is sold subject to the condition that it shall not, by way of trade or otherwise, be lent, resold, hired out, stored in a retrieval system, or otherwise circulated without the publisher's prior consent in any form of binding or cover other than that in which it is published and without a similar condition including this condition being imposed on the subsequent purchaser.

ISBN: 978-1-911343-61-5

Yeoyu ——
new voices

4

1

Years ago, she dreamt she was getting a divorce. She was in high school, it was exam week and she'd fallen asleep at her desk with her head tucked in the crook of her arm. She remained a schoolgirl in the dream, with the same bobbed hair and grey uniform, but *[text obscured by torn/overlaid slip]* ned on his heels and walk*[...]* the tie around his neck w*[...]*

KIM SOOM

There was a notebook open on her desk that day, a fragment from one of Emily Dickinson's letters scribbled between trigonometry equations: *I never have taken a peach in my Hand so late in the Year*... Emily Dickinson, who, she'd heard, had remained celibate her entire life and whose headstone read, simply, *Called back*.

Much later, she confessed to her work colleagues that she'd once dreamt of divorcing a man in a striped, navy necktie. It was over lunch at a dumpling place near the office. Youngmi sonbe was with them, but showed little interest and continued to eat her *mandu* soup in silence. But another colleague asked her how she'd felt – the one who was attending a series of lectures on Freudian psychoanalysis.

'I don't think I made much of it,' she said but admitted that, since that day, any man in a dark blue tie, glimpsed on the subway or on a bus, reminded her of that dream. What she didn't say was that the man in the dream had been her father.

Peaches were her mother's favourite fruit. But, that particular year, she would not see her mother hold a peach; not even once, as the summer waxed and waned. Nor would she the following summer.

The years passed.

DIVORCE

2

The waiting area of Room 204 lacks windows. Where a window should be, there is a door with a few dozen yellow plastic chairs with backrests lined up theatre-style to face it. There are almost no empty seats. The heating is on full blast and the air is dry and stuffy, but she doesn't take off her wool coat.

She sits towards the back of the room as a man in a grey jacket and woman in a knitted maroon coat emerge through the open door. The woman looks calm. She bears the expression of someone who's finally got through what needed getting through. She holds a sheet of paper in her hand. The man looks flustered, his face flushed. Evading glances, they hurry away as, over the speaker, a woman's voice calls out the name of another couple.

Kim Songmin ssi, Seo Heekyong ssi.

The voice is a routine one: neither soft nor booming, thin nor deep. It's neither overtly clipped, nor is it friendly.

A man in the second row bustles to his feet. The woman next to him with shoulders tensed rises slowly, like a corn being removed. The man looks at the woman with contempt before striding off. The woman follows and the door shuts behind them.

She closes her eyes and follows sounds: the further opening ...tting of the door punctuated by the calling out of names, ... the floor, the gurgling of the water cooler, the rustling of papers, the banging of a stapler, the drone of a phone.

When she finally reopens her eyes, the clock is pointing to twenty-past ten. She arrived at just past twenty-to. Cholsik showed up half an hour later.

Everyone in the waiting room wears their own look of unease veiled under a thin layer of nonchalance. They vary in age. From a woman who appears so youthful she could pass for a middle-school student to hoary older men. They stare at their phones, gaze vacantly at the middle distance, or sneak looks around them. Everyone is careful not to let their eyes meet.

Cholsik, glued to the screen of his smartphone, grumbles, 'Apparently divorce after death is the new fad in Japan...'

She remembers reading something about this in yesterday's paper. She had assumed from the headline that the article was about divorces filed by surviving spouses after the death of their partners, the term 'divorce after death' conjuring in her mind a divorce between the living and the dead. As it turned out, the term referred to people divorcing not their dead spouses but the family of their dead spouses. Hand in an application for the Termination of Familial Relations to the relevant authorities, and you could dissolve all legal ties from your in-laws. According to the article, this was occurring at such alarming rates in Japan it bordered on becoming a trend.

'Once you're dead it's all over anyway – what's the point?' Cholsik mutters.

'It may be over for one, but it isn't for the other one, is it – '

'You think we'll be done by eleven? I'm meeting someone at noon,' Cholsik speaks over her in a dry voice.

'You couldn't have pushed it back a couple of hours? Or postponed? What if you're late...?'

DIVORCE

She doesn't ask who he's meeting.

'They say it only takes a couple of minutes.'

Her eyes land on a grey-haired man. Next to him sits a woman whose voluminous hair, dyed a burgundy red, is likely a wig. How long had they lived as husband and wife, now? Forty years? Fifty?

'If you haven't yet handed in your IDs, please do so now,' announces the man sitting guard at a desk by the door. His voice is business-like to the point of peremptoriness. He glares at a man in a blue baseball cap for a few seconds before gathering up the sheaves of paper on his desk. The man in the cap is snickering with a young woman at whatever it is they're watching on the woman's phone screen. The way they're dressed, they could be university students out on a date at the cinema or café on a weekday afternoon. They look giddy, but also somewhat glum, like kids summoned to the staff room.

Again the voice calls out a pair of names. A man, balding at the front, and a woman with tight curls get to their feet and head toward Room 204. *Confirmation of Intent for Divorce by Mutual Consent*, says a sign on the door. Nine pairs have already entered and left the room.

'When do they plan on calling us?' A male voice with a thick Gyeongsang-Province accent booms across the room.

The word 'us' on the lips of a complete stranger jolts her: it feels intrusive and aggressive. She shakes her head without realising what she's doing.

'When do they plan on calling us, I say?'

'When it's our turn,' says the woman next to him.

They bicker. Listening, she wonders how much longer they will go on referring to themselves as a unit.

A stout, pot-bellied man hurries into the waiting room. He

trails a thick cloud of perfume. After a second, he shakes his head violently, like someone who's realised he's entered the wrong train compartment, and rushes out again. A woman raises her hand belatedly as if to wave then bolts to her feet and clacks after him in heels. The sound of their raised voices crashes back into the waiting room. Ignoring the fuss, Cholsik asks in a hoarse voice, 'Did you get some sleep last night?'

'More or less...' she mutters. In fact, she didn't get a wink.

She could have not shown up today. Or Cholsik could have not shown up. But she did, as did he. That they both showed up is what counts.

●

Seven years ago, during the time of her mastectomy and chemotherapy, Cholsik was working in a city down south photographing non-regular labourers who'd been terminated without cause from a shipyard. Cholsik had already spent several years capturing their faces since switching to documentary photography after working as a photographer for a daily newspaper. When her chemo ended, her doctor proposed a regimen of radiation treatments and a round of hormonal drugs. This was customary, to prevent the cancer from recurring, but she wouldn't be able to conceive during treatment and, throughout the subsequent months, she suffered from irregular periods and insomnia. After an agonising interval of weeks where she was unable to sleep for more than a few hours each night, she finally consulted her doctor who referred her to a psychiatrist. Not long after, Cholsik returned home after two months away and asked, as if reminded by a passing thought, 'So I suppose the treatment's going well?'

As she searched for an adequate response, he asked further, again as if it was news to him, 'And how long did you say you had

DIVORCE

to take the hormones for?'
'Well, about five years...'
'Five? So not for the rest of your life, then?'
The next day, he headed south again.

Another time, while still on these treatments, she accompanied Cholsik to the opening of an exhibition. Choi was a well-known documentary photographer and a passionate mentor. His wife and their two adult sons were also present. During the evening, Choi made a speech and started it by praising his wife at some length: this elegant woman, a tireless partner and the wise mother of his children, who managed the household on his behalf, him being a known scoundrel and all, what an excellent job she'd done of raising their two sons – that sort of thing. He described further how she had attended to all familial matters, big and small, on his side of the family, how, as the eldest daughter-in-law, she had taken on the responsibility of nursing her father-in-law back to health. As Choi glanced at his wife in admiration and gratitude, she felt as though she might suffocate, knowing the extent to which he had been a burden on the woman. There had been whispered rumours of how she, presently flanked by her two handsomely tall sons, had had to half-drag the student he'd impregnated to a clinic for a secret abortion. Choi went on to thank his guests for their attendance.

Once the official part of the evening was done and as she examined the photographs on the wall, Choi's wife materialised at her side.

'Isn't it our job to understand them, after all?'
'I'm sorry, our job...?'
'As wives, I mean. It helps me to think of him as a delinquent son rather than a husband. Makes me more tolerant. I find there's not much I can't understand or forgive when I do. Don't mothers

protect their sons, even the murderous ones, whatever the cost? You and I both chose difficult men, so what else can we do? It's an old-fashioned thing to say, I know, but it's our lot...'

Stifling the urge to retort that she hadn't married a grown man in order to mother him, she turned back to the photograph in front of her. On a low-lying green hill stood a nude woman, her dark and ample bush in full view. The title was *Lilith*, and it had a surrealist touch unlike Choi's previous work. The composition had been shot with a shortened perspective and it took a second for her to realise that the woman in the two-dimensional rendition was wearing a prosthetic leg. It was contrived to the point of being repulsive.

Later, in the taxi home, Cholsik muttered, 'You see how hyongsunim is...?'

He called Choi's wife 'hyongsunim', as though she were the wife of an older brother. It was only as they were waiting for the light to change at a crossroads that she realised what Cholsik had meant.

Getting out of the taxi and heading toward a side alley as dark and narrow as an ink cartridge, she said to Cholsik, almost in warning, 'Don't you dare force that on me...'

If only he hadn't titled it *Lilith*, she thought, later. That might have saved it.

●

The woman seated across from her now fidgets with her phone. Her permed hair has lost its curl, and, worn loose and wild, it gives her a distraught look. She'd seen her earlier, when stopping by the restroom before making her way into the waiting area, and had heard her talking on her phone by the mirrors.

'And when I told him I was planning to divorce my husband,

DIVORCE

do you know what he said? *Do you know what he said?* Life's complicated enough, why complicate it even more if you can help it – surely it can't be that bad. *If I can help it? Can't be that bad?* He's smiling as he says it, but does he realise that this is one of the worst things anyone's said to me? It is that bad, why else would I want one in the first place? But he'd rather I live to see a hundred playing house with a cheat of a husband who swaps mistresses like they're yearly calendars? What about his Facebook posts? All those pro-fem comments? Has he been *pretending* all this time?'

Feeling her gaze, the woman twisted her neck to glance back. Outlined heavily, her eyes resembled those of an animal in fear for its life.

Caught off guard, she smiled at the woman, but was met by a frosty look of warning.

'It's not easy, is it...' she mumbled under her breath. Words she'd once heard Youngmi sonbe utter at the end of a phone call. Though her voice was barely louder than a whisper, the woman seemed to hear her.

Sure enough, her lips twitched open.

'No, it's not easy...' she thought she heard the woman say, and she felt the rims of her own eyes grow wide.

●

She saw Youngmi sonbe again two summers ago, after having lost touch for close to ten years. Youngmi had been her supervisor at her first job at the P. Welfare Foundation but had moved to Youngdong in North Chungcheong Province some years previously. She'd requested a half-day's leave and headed to the bus terminal in Gangnam to buy a ticket to Youngdong without so much as a phone call. It was an unusually hot summer and in the swelter the fruit shops reeked of overripe peaches.

Her hormone treatment was nearing its end by this time and she'd turned down a commission, though it was the first she'd had in nearly a year – her sentences still refused to become poetry. On the trip over, she dwelt on how she'd discarded her given name early in her literary career when her work was first selected for publication in a literary magazine. She'd written a brief author's note as requested and signed it with a pen name. And in that moment she'd understood why she'd been so intent on becoming published: she had sought to shed the name her father had given her and find her own.

Once at Youngdong Terminal, she stopped to grab a roll of *gimbap* for a late lunch and only then did she put in a call. Youngmi sonbe sounded surprisingly composed for someone who'd just received word from an old colleague she hadn't heard from in a decade.

'I've been meaning to get away and clear my head, and today I suddenly thought of you, sonbe. I'd heard that you were in Youngdong now... I really wanted to see you... I got your phone number from Sonju sonbe.'

Youngmi said simply, 'I'm glad you came.'

An hour or so later, they were both seated in a café in Youngdong's town centre. Youngmi had invited her to her home, which was near the university, but she had dissembled and said instead that, no, she could really use a cup of coffee.

She returned Youngmi's calm gaze.

'I wanted to see how you were doing, sonbe...'

She had changed. There were lines around her eyes and mouth and it had softened the general impression of her face, which had tended previously to appear cold and distant. Her long hair was tied loosely at the nape and her pale blue cotton dress, with its

DIVORCE

smattering of tiny flowers, gave her a relaxed air. The Youngmi sonbe she remembered had gravitated towards simple but sophisticated clothes in neutral tones.

'I'm sorry I didn't call sooner.'

'Nonsense. I should have called you. I'm ashamed I didn't —'

'— Sonbe, I'm sorry.'

'For what?'

'For keeping my distance when it must have been so difficult...' She couldn't believe that she was bringing up events now ten years old. 'I'd heard some gossip about you... Not that I believed everything I heard...'

A few months before the rumours of Youngmi and her affair with Ko, the Overseas Programmes Division Head, had started doing the rounds, Youngmi had surprised her colleagues by divorcing her husband. The surprise was due, in part, to the fact that she had never let slip she was in any way dissatisfied with her marriage. She herself had assumed Youngmi to be happy and had had dinner with her and her husband on two occasions. She'd found him to be a reasonable, well-mannered person.

Youngmi's image – tidy, impeccable – had been trashed, first by the divorce, then the scandal. The Chairman of the Board for P. Welfare Foundation was, at eighty-five years old, a respected elder of a big church who, in the speeches he gave at the beginning of every year, would expound upon the importance of living by The Commandments. Rumours of the affair soon reached his ears. He was livid and promptly fired her. To fire only one of the two people involved – the woman – was, of course, unfair, but nobody had voiced their objections or questioned the decision, despite the Foundation's overwhelming majority of female employees. Ko volunteered to go overseas, and, upon his return three years later, received a promotion, then became Director of the Foundation's Community Welfare Centre.

'I didn't realise until much later that the rumours had been grossly exaggerated...'

Once back from his stint overseas, Ko had belatedly offered an explanation about the scandal: 'Turns out, sometimes there can be smoke without a fire,' he'd said with a sheepish smile. The rumours that cost Youngmi sonbe her job were about as inconvenient to him as gum on the sole of his shoe or muddy water on his suit pants.

'Why didn't you say something at the time?'

At her question Youngmi's eyes flickered, though not, it seemed, out of resentment.

'Nobody asked me about it.'

'I'm sorry, sonbe.'

'About five years after the divorce, I ran into my ex-husband by chance at Kyobo Bookstore. He had a baby in his arms. I'd heard that he'd remarried. That night, I called him for the first time since our divorce. There was something I had to ask him. I felt I couldn't get on with my life before hearing the answer...'

Youngmi lifted her glass and took two slow sips. The ice had all but melted in the water.

'We had married on the condition that we wouldn't start a family. He had told me he didn't want to waste his life on children as our parents' generation had. It wasn't a one-sided demand, either. It terrified me to imagine the planet in another hundred years' time. Depleted resources, irregular weather patterns, every day hundreds more children dead due to water shortages... So incredibly bleak. But I also knew that I would nonetheless want children one day. I thought he would too, once he was a bit older, but even after twelve years of marriage his position hadn't changed. On our way back from the first birthday of one of his

DIVORCE

nephews, I told him I wanted kids. It was the first time I'd said it. He didn't utter a single word the entire drive home. Not until a few days later did he finally say, almost as an afterthought, while mixing Japanese curry into his rice, that during his lunch break that day he'd gone to a nearby urologist's office and had a vasectomy. I was in complete shock. I didn't want it to show so I just sat there, shoving food into my mouth. And then to find out, years later, that he was now not only remarried but had reversed his vasectomy...'

'...'

'I don't understand what being married means any more. If we'd had children would our marriage have survived? My mother seems to think so. I'm not so sure. Perhaps we would have stayed together then, but whether that has any meaning in itself... I used to wake up in the middle of the night and grab his hand. Because of how distant he seemed, this person asleep at my side, as if he was not of this world.'

'...'

'We were married in the presence of family and friends, we registered our marriage at the district office, we were officially husband-and-wife; yet in twelve years together we didn't share a single day as partners – that's what I realised.'

'You didn't find it hard to live on your own?'

'It's not so bad, really...'

'What are you doing for work?'

'I'm an after-school tutor. I opened a centre in Seoul before moving here, but one of the parents learned my marital status – I didn't see a reason to lie – and pretty soon the students stopped coming. I spent a year not working. I sent out my CV, but I'd only get as far as the interviews. Finally I saw a notice in the window of a *gamjatang* restaurant, looking for servers. I went in to ask about the terms, the owner asked me if I could start right away, so I said yes...'

'You worked at a *gamjatang* place?'

Youngmi sonbe had graduated from one of the so-called 'elite' universities. Having joined the Foundation straight out of uni, Youngmi had won the trust of the then-Director of the Community Relief Centre. That the Director had wanted Youngmi sonbe as his daughter-in-law had been an open secret.

'I had to make a living somehow... By the way, how is your mother these days?'

●

It had only been her second month at the Foundation when her sixty-five-year-old father had lain into her sixty-year-old mother until her eardrum burst. When she'd answered the call around ten in the morning, her mother hadn't been able to say a single word and simply whimpered over the phone. Fearing the worst, she'd hurriedly checked with Youngmi sonbe before heading home to Inchon.

She'd found her mother lying prone on the kitchen floor, clasping her bloodied ear.

'I don't want... I can't live with your father any more...'

He was a high-school Korean teacher and regarded his wife, a middle-school graduate, as an inferior in every way. He was in charge of all household decisions and finances. Her mother received an allowance for living costs and had to submit the budget book to him every month as though she were a student getting her homework checked. He disallowed the smallest indulgence, not even a scarf that might have caught her eye.

After that day, she'd set to work at once preparing her parents' divorce and without informing her older brothers, both

DIVORCE

of whom married early and had by now started their own families. She'd sought counsel at a law office near City Hall Station and learned how one might go about filing. When she'd explained to her mother that, if they were to go ahead, she would receive a portion of her father's assets and pension as alimony, her mother had looked at her with wide-eyed disbelief. In all her life she had never even owned a bank account in her name.

When she finally approached her father with the legal papers he was lounging on the living room sofa in his pyjamas in front of the evening news. Her mother was at the dining table sorting bean sprouts.

Reaching for the glass bowl laden with nuts, he glanced down at her hand.

'What?'

'These are papers for your divorce, yours and mother's. Mother wants a divorce.'

Her father's face turned scarlet, then a little blue. As she explained further, he picked up the glass bowl and hurled it to the floor, shattering it and spraying nuts in every direction.

'Forty years of this isn't enough for you?' she demanded.

'What?'

'Forty years of cursing, beating, treating her like a slave and you're still not satisfied?'

'She should know she's lived in the lap of luxury, safe from the dangers of the world for forty years, all thanks to me!'

'If that's how you see it, then we have no choice but to file for divorce.'

'Your cunt of a mother put you up to this?'

He lunged forward and grabbed her by the hair. She tried to squirm free and he punched her in the face, splitting her lip. She could feel blood trickle down her chin, but her father wouldn't let up. It took her mother wielding a kitchen knife and yelling in his ear for him to finally let go of her hair.

'Don't hit her! It's my fault... I'm to blame. Don't hit her...'

She looked over at her mother and shook her head.

'It's all my doing... please don't hit her. What if you leave a mark on her face? She's not a child any more...'

'Know this,' he hissed in her ear, 'the day we divorce will be the day of your cow of a mother's funeral.'

He glared at them before storming off to the master bedroom. She walked over to her mother, who trembled, one hand still gripped round the handle of the kitchen knife.

'You haven't done anything wrong, Mum...'

'It's all because of me...'

During her third year of primary school, she'd brought home a classmate. She hadn't realised it was exam week, which meant her father would be home earlier than usual. Usually, when she brought friends over, her mother would make them potato pancakes or vegetable fritters. But that day she couldn't find her mother in the yard or in the kitchen and out on the *maru* there was only a solitary fan, turning slowly from left to right. She was about to call out when she heard the sound of a mangled, crumpled voice leaking out from behind her parents' closed bedroom door. *It's my fault, it's my fault...* Words she'd heard her mother utter again and again each time her father raged and lashed out like a rabid street-dog.

'You're not to blame for anything... stop saying that. You have to stop saying it's your fault.'

She began looking for a place she and her mother could move to, but as preparations for the divorce continued, the biggest obstacle turned out not to be her father but her mother. At the lawyer's office, she wouldn't say a single word

DIVORCE

in response to questions about her marriage. The lawyer was visibly perturbed and reiterated that it was paramount that she express her willingness to proceed before filing. They stopped by a *nengmyun* restaurant for a late lunch on the way back home and still she maintained her stubborn silence. Watching her mother fish out the stringy noodles from the bowl of cold, pale broth, she asked:

'Mum, don't you want this?'

'...'

'You said. You said it was what you wanted.'

'I... I'm not sure...'

'Remember that time you brought home a potted dahlia from the market? Around my second year of middle school? Remember how Father scolded you like you were a child for being reckless with your money? You said to me then, you said once I was old enough you'd divorce him, even if you had to make a living as a domestic...'

Her mother's eyes clouded over. She realised that her mother no longer knew her own mind.

She tried a different approach. 'Mum, how do you feel right now?'

'Hmm...?'

'How would you describe how you feel right now? Are you sad?'

'...'

'Happy?'

'...'

'Angry?'

'...'

'Don't you feel angry?'

'I don't know...'

'Don't you feel so angry you might go mad?'

KIM SOOM

Kang Ilgu ssi, Lim Soon-im ssi...

An old man groans and strains to get to his feet as the woman next to him stands up and straightens her clothes. He walks with a slight limp, heading not for the door but toward the desk. He asks something of the man guarding it.

'You should speak to the judge about it.'

'But I've got something to say!'

'Yes, and I say go speak to the judge.'

The old woman throws him a disapproving look before disappearing though the doorway.

'Fifty-three years, all told...'

Cholsik tears his eyes away from his phone and looks over.

'Not five, not ten... *fifty-three years* as husband and wife.'

The woman seated diagonally across bolts from her chair without warning and runs out into the corridor, trailing a clattering echo of heels. A few moments later, the sound of her exasperated voice floods back into the waiting room.

'Where are you? Where the hell are you? Grab a taxi and get here *right this moment*. You want to go to trial? You *promised*. In front of the kids, you promised, you said you would consent, you wrote it all down on paper, remember? Why won't you let me go, do you mean to hold onto my ankle for the rest of your life like some demented dog?'

The woman's voice chokes, close to a sob.

She recalls a woman who was so desperate to divorce her husband she'd contemplated suicide. They'd met during chemotherapy. Her husband was the pastor of a church that had a congregation of roughly two thousand and he was convinced she was neither faithful nor praying enough given her role as a

DIVORCE

pastor's wife. Whenever he judged her to have acted or spoken in front of the congregation in a manner unbefitting of the dignity of her role, he would quietly summon her to his office. He would then lower the blinds, lock the door and strike her head three or four times with the flat of his palm. When she'd confessed to her husband that she had breast cancer, he had chastised her and told her she was being punished for her lack of faith and prayer. Despite being gripped by a terrible fear that if she didn't divorce him, cancer cells would spread through her body and kill her all the faster – a fear that, at its worst, gripped her at one or two minute intervals – in the end, she was unable to go through with it. It would mean divorcing the congregation, two thousand faithful followers, she said; it was tantamount to divorcing God. So she vacillated, unable to shake off her husband's image and judgement. She had texted recently to say her cancer had metastasised to her spine.

●

Ultimately, the plan to orchestrate her mother's divorce had come to nothing: 'I've got to marry you off first, haven't I,' her mother had said, finally, in a faltering voice. 'If the man's family finds out your parents are divorced...'

She had cajoled and insisted, and then, realising there was nothing more she could do as long as her mother remained unwilling, had told her she was washing her hands of the whole matter. A few months later, she'd left home and found a bedsit near work. The day of the move, she had been giddy at having escaped finally, but also left regretting the harshness of her words to her mother.

About ten days after her visit to Youngdong, she received a call from Youngmi sonbe who said she'd dreamt about her since their meeting. She didn't explain further and started talking instead about the *gamjatang* restaurant where she'd worked. She described the drunk men who'd grab her ass and make her jump; the times she'd spilled food while carrying the heavy pots to the tables; how the owner's husband had started hitting on her when he found out she was a divorcée.

'I'd wrap up for the day and get back home, and it would be past midnight. I barely had the strength to wash my makeup off, I'd sit and stare at the TV before collapsing into bed. Sometimes I'd wake up in the middle of the night and think about how it was all over for me, my life as well as my womanhood...'

'...'

'My menopause had just started – quite early...'

'...'

'D'you know, Minjong ssi, I was on my way somewhere in the dream. By bus... The driver was missing both his arms. The bus stopped at some point, though there was no stop sign, and then you got on...'

Youngmi fell silent.

After some seconds, she went on: 'Say there's a woman who one day became senile. The woman's husband remained devoted and took care of her, even as her condition deteriorated and she was no longer able to recognise herself. Then say the woman, who was losing her memories, went in search of her former husband, having completely erased her current husband of over forty years. She went looking for the husband she'd left more than four decades earlier, believing him to be her husband still...'

'It's not easy, is it...' Youngmi said before ending the call.

DIVORCE

To mark her mother's seventieth birthday, Cholsik took a portrait. Her mother wore the pale pink blouse she'd given her as a present and there was a pot of yellow chrysanthemums by her side. But she seemed to find it difficult to face the camera. Each time the shutter clicked, her shoulders tensed reflexively. Eventually Cholsik managed to capture her looking directly at the lens. When she first saw the print, she couldn't help breathing a sigh of relief. Or perhaps it was more an exclamation. Her mother's face as pictured, in black and white, seemed so much sadder than in her mind's eye.

'What do you suppose it's like to be impregnated by a man who curses and assaults you like a malicious pimp?' she said to Cholsik. 'And to then give birth to and raise that child? Could she ever love the child, seeing the same glint in its eyes...?' For in her brothers' eyes she sometimes saw her father's, as in her own.

'What are you talking about?'

'And not just one child, but three...'

She remembered a time her father had bundled up the family into his first car, a silver-grey Daewoo Remans, and driven all the way to Gyungpodae Beach in the eastern coastal city of Gangneung for the day. It was their first and last family outing.

At one of the raw fish restaurants that lined the beach, her mother had grabbed a perilla leaf as soon as the plate of freshly filleted flounder arrived. She placed it over the throbbing gills as if to hide the little fish heart beating below the surface.

Over the course of the meal, her father managed to empty an entire bottle of *soju*. Then he climbed into the driver's seat to drive them back to Seoul. As they were approaching Daegwallyeong Pass, a set of glowing blue eyes briefly appeared against the ink-black darkness of the road ahead before vanishing under the silver-grey Remans. The car shook. Her mother, who had been keeping a wary eye on her father throughout, covered her face as his foot bore down on the accelerator. As the car sped through a tunnel, her mother finally burst into tears. Father slammed his fists down on the wheel. 'Stop blubbing, you cunt, you'll bring me bad luck!'

She saw the covered heart of the fish again, its tiny shudder barely concealed under the green leaf. She saw her mother cowering in fear. In that moment, it had seemed as if all of the world's violence sprung from her father. All the violence perpetrated in the world, big and small – it all seemed to have originated from him.

●

She'd always hoped her mother would outlive her father, even by one day. She'd thought that in that way at least her mother might briefly be free. But when he finally died, her mother also suffered a rapid decline, both physically and psychologically, becoming hypertensive and eventually suffering a cerebral haemorrhage. Throughout her mother's operation and subsequent convalescence, she stayed by her side. She didn't mention her own surgery, as they still hadn't properly made up since her failed attempts to initiate her mother's divorce.

It was a four-bed recovery room, but occasionally she and her mother would have it to themselves. On one such occasion, she quietly dabbed at her mother's hands with a moistened gauze towel, thinking her asleep. After a while, her mother opened her eyes to peer at the ceiling and said, in a distant voice, 'I did run away, you know...'

'Wh – you mean from Father?'

'Twice, in fact...'

'When?'

DIVORCE

'Not even a year into our marriage.'

She could feel her mother's bony hands stiffen, her fingers as frail as bird's legs.

'I couldn't stomach living with someone who used such foul language. Not even my own parents spoke to me the way he did, and they treated me worse than a pig. They didn't have much affection for him, either... But, one day, I washed and hung up the laundry and simply left. I made my way to Gimchon. It wasn't such a short distance in those days, Inchon to Gimchon. I left when it was light and reached my parents' after sunset. "I can't live like that," I said, and your grandmother just nodded. But somehow a distant relative — in fact, the one who arranged our marriage — got wind of my whereabouts and contacted your father.'

'And the second time?'

'That was the year before you were born, when your brothers were ten and nine. I left them with your grandmother and headed straight for the bus terminal. She probably suspected as much, because she asked me where I was going. I lied and told her I was off to the market to buy some fish, but I couldn't look her in the eyes, I was trembling so much. I got to the terminal and bought the first ticket I could, a bus headed to Gwangju, Jeolla Province... I arrived in Gwangju where, of course, I didn't know a soul so I hung about the terminal for a bit then went into a *baekban* restaurant and asked for work. The elderly woman who owned the place said sure. Eunmi, it was called... Eunmi Restaurant. I'd cry every night at the thought of your brothers, but still I couldn't go back...'

As she pictured her mother working at Eunmi Restaurant, an image of Youngmi quietly superimposed, the two women merging in silhouette.

A patient was wheeled into the room from surgery, which

brought her mother's story to an abrupt end. The nurse instructed the patient's guardian on next steps: keep an eye on her and make sure she didn't fall asleep again after anaesthesia had worn off. The guardian – a short, greying man – nodded and did as he was told.

'Yeobo, open your eyes. Yeobo, yeobo... You did well... Yeobo, you have to keep your eyes open... They say the surgery went well... Very well, they said...'

Her mother watched the couple enviously, her lips sealed. On discharge, she refused all her children and their invitations to stay and insisted instead on returning home alone.

DIVORCE

3

During the one-month deliberation period in which they were supposed to think things over, Cholsik made yet another trip to the shipyard. He went out around nine in the evening after receiving a call and it was sometime after midnight when she received a text message. Something urgent had come up and he was on a night bus headed south, it said.

He didn't return for three days, then unexpectedly he was back at the kitchen table, as if he'd flown in with the night, a bag of sandwich bread, a carton of milk and a jar of peanut butter in front of him. The clock on the table read 2:15am.

'I was famished...' Cholsik laughed glumly, gesturing at the slice of bread in his hand. His chin was dark. She realised he hadn't shaved while he was away. The bread had been in the fridge for some time; it must have been cold and hard and stale.

It occurred to her then that this was a pattern with him: He'd reappear unannounced in the dead of night or at the crack of dawn and the first thing he'd do was rummage around in the kitchen for something to eat as if he'd starved for days.

She cleared her throat. 'There's *mandu*, shall I steam some for you?'

'That could work...'

KIM SOOM

She retrieved the dumplings from the freezer and placed them in the steamer, turned on the gas stove, boiled water in the electric kettle.

As the water started to bubble, Cholsik spoke. 'I heard Kang Ingu ssi died...'

Pouring hot water into a mug, she turned the name Kang Ingu over in her mind. She knew nobody by that name. 'Who was he again?'

'One of the non-regulars at the shipyard. He modelled for me,' he said flatly. 'A woman called me, his wife, saying she'd asked several people for my number. She needed a photo of him for the wake, and was wondering if I might give some of mine to use.'

He'd gone all that way just to hand over a funeral photo to a dead man's wife.

'I thought I might as well stay until the morning of the procession before heading back.'

She dropped a bag of jasmine tea into her mug, carried it over to the table and sat across from him.

'I took hundreds of photos, mostly of his face. At least six hundred since the day I first met him. He'd come to the shipyard for his job interview. I trailed behind him everywhere after that day, capturing his face over and over. It became almost nauseating.'

She imagined her husband's camera lens trained on the visage of some man called Kang Ingu at the precise moment beam radiation was targeting the tumour in her left breast.

'The interviewer was the foreman of the company subcontracted by the shipyard. They hadn't been allotted office space within the compound, so the interview took place in the snack bar next to the canteen. The foreman asked Kang how long he thought he could bear the work. When Kang didn't answer, the foreman glanced at my lens and muttered, "Cause I've seen them

DIVORCE

all. Disappearing after a half-day's work, not a word of notice, chickening out even before they've begun or as soon as they've put on the uniform." "So you reckon you're up to it," the foreman asked. Kang nodded, and the interview was over. He had zero experience or skills, but he was expected to fix all the electrical wiring in the ships' internal circuitry...'

The smell of steaming *mandu* wafted from the pot. It brought to mind highway pit stops and numerous snacks wolfed down in the middle of the night. It was well past 3:00 am: too early a time for some, far too late for others. She told herself that presently they would be back in the car and on the road; that they'd come upon the tunnel just as first light dawned.

'He had a face that never seemed to change, never altered its expression. If it wasn't for his eyes and the slight tremor I saw in them, I felt like I might have tried to rip it off with my bare hands. He bore the work for four months, then vanished. Not a word to anyone, not even to me, when I'd been his shadow for all those weeks and months.'

She stood up, turned the stove off and lifted the lid of the steamer. She returned to the table with the plate of dumplings.

'He had nothing to say to me, nothing he could tell me about himself, in all the time I had my camera on him. Never mentioned how he ended up at a shipyard. Never chatted to anyone or tried to make friends. He was completely solitary, he might as well have dropped out of the sky one night like a shooting star.'

Cholsik made as if to eat, then paused. He continued: 'There were moments when I felt like I was swallowing up his face... Every time I pressed the shutter, in fact. And that face – it looked like someone had driven two or three dozen nails into it.'

He started chewing. She imagined he was chewing the face of Kang Ingu, that if she were to peer inside his mouth she'd find it there, grotesquely mangled and slick with saliva.

'It was only through his wife that I was able to learn something about him. I meant to head straight back after giving her the photograph, but the place was so deserted I couldn't bring myself to leave. He did have two older sisters, but someone said they'd emigrated to Germany a long time ago. I had a chance to talk to his wife the day before the funeral. She thought he and I had been close. Not an unreasonable assumption, given I'd kept vigil for three days. She asked me something. She asked if I'd known that they were separated.'

'For the first ten years they'd apparently been the couple everyone envied. The year their twin sons turned six, she'd gone to Australia on a two-year language course, taking the children with her. And that's when there seems to have been a lot of upheaval at the steel-manufacturing company where Kang worked. Subsidiaries taken over, extensive layoffs, and Kang in charge of the firing. Nearly three hundred factory workers were let go. One of them took his own life. And then his widow came to see Kang, carrying an infant on her back...'

Cholsik's story was not unfamiliar to her.

'When she returned after her studies, she found her husband entirely changed. She said that once, while she and the kids were still in Australia, Kang had called her at two in the morning. He'd asked her, all serious and without a word of explanation, what she thought about moving to Australia permanently. She'd balked at the prospect, told him he had to stay put and make it to retirement, or at least until he was promoted to director-level. If he cared at all about his wife, his children, their happiness, he should stop that nonsense at once; he'd better be prepared to bury his bones in that company.'

'Well, she couldn't have known what he was going through...'

DIVORCE

She found herself reflexively defensive.

'He resigned, though. Resigned and used his severance package to invest in stocks, only to lose everything. Then there was a big row, the neighbours from across the hall called the apartment's security on them, and Kang started to burn all their family photos. Locked himself in the bathroom and burned every single one in the basin, apparently, including ones from the wedding...'

'Which is why she didn't have a photo for the wake.'

'Yeah.'

'That's one good thing at least. That you had a photo they could use.'

She found herself engrossed in thoughts about this city in the south she'd never visited. It was only when she heard the whistling of a pressure rice cooker coming from a neighbouring kitchen that she realised morning had dawned.

'Hey. Do we have to get divorced?' said Cholsik suddenly, spitting out the words as if dusting away sand from the tip of his tongue.

●

She first brought up her wish three years ago. It was winter, she was still undergoing hormone therapy and the insomnia had gotten so extreme she was unable to sleep for more than thirty minutes at a time.

There had been a cold weather alert and after work she'd had to attend the year-end work dinner. She got home around midnight to find that she'd misplaced her keys and couldn't open the door. She called Cholsik at least two dozen times, but he wouldn't pick up. For two hours, she waited for him to call back, shivering in the stairwell of their building; eventually, she found a Lotteria that was open all night and sat drinking coffee as she waited for day to break. He had left for Miryang in North Gyeongsang Province three days previously, on assignment for a special feature for a current affairs magazine and was due back that day.

Staring through the fast-food restaurant window at the empty pedestrian crossing, she recalled how Cholsik hadn't been at her side when she'd had a miscarriage a year into their marriage, or when the man downstairs had pounded on their door in the middle of the night to complain about a leak in the bathroom ceiling. He hadn't been there the time she'd had to call a repairman to come and fix the boiler or the time she'd gone from building to building looking for a new flat because their lease was up. Nor had he been there the day she'd had an appointment at the ObGyn to find out why she hadn't been able to get pregnant after the miscarriage. Indeed, there were times when she wanted to ask him how someone so committed to communicating and connecting with the socially disadvantaged, to documenting their suffering in painstaking detail, could be so unfeeling to the suffering of the person closest to him.

When he finally called at 6:00am. it was to inform her that he planned to stay a few more day. She could hear no trace of alcohol or sleep in his voice. She told him she wanted a divorce on his return ten days later. In lieu of a response, he complained that she had changed the lock on their door without consulting him. She brought up the subject again several times thereafter, only to be ignored. Until one night he returned home drunk enough to slur his words and demanded, 'You, what do you write poetry for?'

'What?'

'Poetry. Why do you write it? Hmm?'

When she responded with frosty silence, he pressed her further. 'Isn't it to save people's souls?'

DIVORCE

'Save people's *souls*... ? I want a divorce, that's all.'
'Doesn't that mean you want to abandon me?'
'Abandon you? What are you talking about?'
'That's what you're doing!'
'Who said anything about abandoning you? I'm talking about a divorce.'
'Isn't that the same thing? If you abandon me, you're as good as abandoning a person's soul. So anything you write from now on is a lie, it may as well be rubbish.'

●

Before she started primary school, her mother took her to visit her grandmother in Gimchon. It was her mother's birthday and her father happened to be away on a three-day school trip. Mother stopped at the market by the intercity bus terminal to buy seaweed, beef, ingredients for *japche* noodles, and some yellow corvine, then, while she played hopscotch and entertained herself in the courtyard, Mother set about cooking, bustling between the kitchen and the water faucet in the yard.

Once the birthday meal was ready, the three women – Grandma, Mother, and she – sat around the laden table. Slipping a spoon into Grandma's hand, Mother said, 'Eat to your heart's content, this is for all you did bringing me into the world.' Grandma spooned rice into her soup bowl and started to eat. After a while her eyes became distant and she began telling them a story.

'There was a woman in the village two hills yonder who was missing both her legs. She'd been missing them since birth... No one thought to wed her even after she came of age, so an old widower brought her to live with him. She may have been missing legs, but she was as tough and as hardworking as anyone. He used to carry her out to the field on his wooden back-rack and she'd spend the entire day tirelessly weeding, using her hands instead of a hoe. And how she devoted herself to him, until this old widower who'd once been riddled with lice glowed and grew all ruddy in the face. They'd been living as husband and wife for six, maybe seven years, when the war broke out. In the chaos, soldiers came to the village saying they were rooting out communist guerrillas and dragged all the men of the village up into the hills. As dusk set in, the sound of guns rattled down. It sounded like they were threshing beans. The next morning, once the soldiers had left the village, the women led their children up the hill. They shouldered their husbands' bodies down to the village, wailing to shake the hills and streams. At her wit's end, the woman without legs crawled up the hill on her arms and, with one arm around his neck, hauled her husband's remains back down the slope, using her other arm to drag herself down the hill...'

'Your soup's getting cold, Mother, you should eat,' Mother said, quietly deboning the fish.

Grandma lifted her spoon to her lips and sighed. 'That's how terrible a thing it is to be husband and wife...'

Her grandfather had passed when Grandma was twenty-six. They were married for six years, but Grandma held *jesa* on the anniversary of his death every year for her remaining thirty-nine years. She came across Grandma's story again in her twenties, in a book about the mass killings that had occurred just before and after the Korean War. Grandma's version of the story was somewhat different from the account recorded in the book, but the broad strokes of it – of village men accused of being communist guerrillas being massacred by the national army, of a woman who didn't have the use of her legs crawling up the mountain to claim her husband's body – these details were the same.

DIVORCE

4

The day her father finally passed away, it occurred to her that if a god did exist then, in her mother, they had granted to her father the worthiest of persons, whom her father had attempted, in the course of their life together, to turn into the lowliest.

●

On the last day of the wake, her mother walked to the altar where her father's framed photo stood, where she crumpled to the floor and started to wail, her cry like silk thread. She asked her mother why she was crying, but her mother only kept repeating, The poor thing, the poor, poor thing...

●

She remembered how on the day they handed in their divorce papers, Cholsik had asked her, 'Am I an orphan now?'
    'An orphan?' she'd repeated, incredulous. 'An orphan?'

●

The night before their divorce, she told Cholsik, recalling their conversation of three years previously, 'I'm not here to save your soul. That's not why I married you.'

KIM SOOM

What she didn't say was that, since his accusation, she hadn't been able to write.

She knew she was troubled by his words. They plagued her, and would likely continue to haunt her for a long time. Perhaps she would never be able to shake them off. She struggled with the state of her own soul as much as anyone else, but this fact didn't lessen the sense of unease.

'I think of this divorce as a rite of passage. Something neither you nor I can avoid. Like a tunnel we've come upon while speeding along the highway...'

'Yes...'

'I hope this rite of passage doesn't bring me unhappiness...'

'Yes, yes...'

'And for you especially, I hope it doesn't bring unhappiness...'

'Yes, yes...'

●

A woman's voice calls out the name of a man and a woman over the speaker. She and Cholsik get to their feet almost simultaneously. Her mouth is parched and she tries to moisten it.

'Are we the last?'

The fragment from Emily Dickinson's letters quoted earlier in this story is from the Korean edition of Anne Carson's Autobiography of Red, Bbalgang-eui Jahsohjon, trans. Seungnam Min, Seoul: Hankyoreh Publishing, 2016.

Yeoyu is a series of chapbooks showcasing the work of some of the most exciting writers working in Korean today, published by Strangers Press, part of the UEA Publishing Project.

여유

Yeoyu is a unique collaboration between an international group of independent creative practitioners, with University of East Anglia, Norwich University of the Arts, and the National Centre for Writing, made possible by LTI Korea.

LTI Korea | N | UEA University of East Anglia | NORWICH UNIVERSITY OF THE ARTS

YEOYU SERIES

1
Five Preludes & A Fugue
Cheon Heerahn
Translated by Emily Yae Won

2
Old Wrestler
Jeon Sungtae
Translated by Sora Kim-Russell

3
Europa
Han Kang
Translated by Deborah Smith

4
Divorce
Kim Soom
Translated by Emily Yae Won

5
Kong's Garden
Hwang Jungeun
Translated by Jeon Seung-Hee

6
Milena, Milena, Ecstatic
Bae Suah
Translated by Deborah Smith

7
Demons
Kang Hwagil
Translated by Mattho Mandersloot

8
Left's Right, Right's Left
Han Yujoo
Translated by Janet Hong